FROM CRITICISM TO GRACE : HER STORY

RIBHA

Made with ♥ on the Notion Press Platform
www.notionpress.com

May I never forget how far You've brought me, Jesus.

"If I didn't have Jesus in my struggles, I wouldn't be as strong as I am today."

Every good and perfect gift comes from God. - James 1:17

Thank You, Jesus!

Contents

Contents

Preface

I am filled with immense joy to place in the hands of the readers my third fiction novella - *'From criticism to Grace : Her Story'*.

This Novella appeared as a result of the undeserving, un-merited and unearned favour *'grace'* in which all of our experiences; good and bad, now serve a purpose, instead of serving shame.

"For by Grace, you have been saved through Faith.
This is not Your doing: It is the gift of God."
- Ephesians 2:8

Acknowledgements

I'm eternally grateful to my readers, for reading and believing in me from the very beginning, for their kindness and support & for their patience.

Writing a book is more rewarding that I could have ever imagined.

'A life of purpose is a life of service, one of my highest privileges, is when I know I'm being used by God to help others.

I'm not a Christian because I'm strong and have it all together, but, because I'm weak and admit I need a Saviour.

Prologue

In God's Timeline

No season is ever wasted in God's Timeline. There's a right season for everything.

Praise God in all circumstances, whether they are good or bad.

God is going to use all of the broken pieces - all the pain, frustration and heartbreak- to make a beautiful masterpiece.

What gives me the most hope everyday is God's grace.

1

Until we meet again

Dad,

No matter how long you've been gone, you'll always be loved and you'll never be forgotten.

I Love You to the heavens and beyond.

Father

[fah-ther] noun

often refers to as a daughter's first love

see also : Superman

'She did not stand alone,
But what stood behind her
The most potent moral force in her life,
Was the love of her father.'

Enter Caption

RIBHA

2

My Father - His Importance in my Life

My father was extraordinary.

I consider myself extremely blessed to have had him in my life.

He was, he is and he will always be, an essential part of my life.

And I'm grateful for everything he had done for me.

I'm filled with immense pride to call him my father.

Whatever the circumstance, he had always been by my side.

He had been my strongest supporter & had consistently been there for me when I needed him.

He was a pillar of strength and wisdom in my life. The love, guidance and selfless support which he provided always prove to be an indelible mark on my journey.

From my early childhood days, I recall his comforting presence.

His confidence in me and my capabilities, gave me the strength to achieve my dreams and reached where I am today.

My father was a very great friend of mine. I respect my father and work to acquire the traits I'll need to be like him as I'm growing older.

He was, he is and he will always be, my real 'Hero'.

3

A Letter to my father in Heaven

A lot of people will tell you that with time, wounds will heal, but unfortunately, the void in your life created by the passing away of your father will never be filled.

However, the great and beautiful thing that will come out of it, is, that you'll truly realize how much he loved you.

My father died when I was twenty-two years old and it was no doubt the hardest time of my life. I label this as the saddest time of my life. We lost the man of the house, we lost our father, he was gone. We would never see him again.

Daddy went to Heaven.

Heaven was a happy place, where he would be able to watch over us. He would be our guardian angel up in the sky. Hence, when I would look up and gaze at the stars, I always thought of him being the brightest star in the sky, shining down.

It is hard to accept that a family of four was meant to be a family of five.

Even though he's gone, I still encourage myself to make him proud.

4

This I believe: In honor of my father, myself & the time we shared.

Growing up, I was known by everyone, as, "daddy's princess".

As my dad passed away suddenly, it came as a great shock to me because I never expected it. The next couple of days, weeks and months, were the hardest I've ever experienced.

When I was diagnosed with Manic Depression, almost everyone stigmatised my mental illness and avoided me. My dad was one of the few people who stood by me through it all. My mental illness was, in a way, a blessing in disguise, as it brought my father and I, closer to each other. Not just that, but, I was also able to choose my father over everyone else. I was able to see myself through my father's eyes which made me realised how much he loved me and how precious I was to him.

With time, even though, my father's untimely death broke my heart, I thought about how sad my dad would be if he knew how I was suffering. I began to accept that he was up in Heaven where I could once again see him. This belief gave me the hope I needed that there was life after death for him in the eternal sense and there was life in me after his death.

The life I began to live after my father's death was full of vitality. I learn to appreciate each moment for how special they are because the next one could be my last.

Enter Caption

5

To Being strong yet again

Today is the day it has all settled inside.

Experiencing some uncertain personal circumstances with my mental health taught me that life can change in an instant. Life can be really great and then really bad in a short period of time.

I'm one of the blessed ones. I realise that. I'm so grateful to God & I'm so grateful for my family.

Sometimes we are taken into troubled waters not to drown but to be cleansed.

Unfortunately, in the fall of 2019, my life made a turn from its usual normalcy to complete haywire, with the sudden demise of my father.

The long story shortened, a couple of days post my father's demise, I was going to have my mid-semester examination, my doctors told me that it would be understandable if I chose to miss it. However, I had successfully given my examination and emerged victorious. Let me say, the support I've had through all of my journeys from my family and my doctors, had been amazing.

Life is unpredictable. Love the people God gave you. Be grateful for everything.

One thing is true : It could always be worse.

6

Take each day as it comes: Living in the moment

All of us are struggling with juggling the chaos of life. Train your mind to be in the present moment - to be in the moment is the *miracle.* Let us not look back in anger, or forward in fear, but around in awareness. When we allow yesterday's pain or the fear of what could happen seep in, we miss everything worth feeling. We should learn to live in the moment with a grateful heart.

Gratitude does not change the scenery, it merely washes clean the glass you look through so you can clearly see the colors.

Jesus was a great example; He was God but yet He still thanked His Father over and over again. Even at The Last Supper while approaching the Cross, He paused to thank the Father.

Gratitude gives us eyes to see God, Love, Beauty, Joy & Abundance. It makes sense of the past, brings peace for today , and, creates a vision for tomorrow.

When I started counting my blessings, life got better.

Today's Mantra: I'm grateful that I'm exactly where I'm meant to be.

7

Every end has a new beginning

And so she said : Let's begin again!

Over the years, I've always held tightly to people I've met, even though I no longer have any meaningful connections other than shared memories. By longing for the past, I've been missing out on the present.

One fine day, I finally realised and learned to let go. Letting go *is not* giving up. Letting go is the pinnacle of enlightened behaviour,

Some things have to end for better things to begin. Forward is the way. Embrace change. Let go.

We can invite 'letting go' when it comes knocking.

<u>Let go. Let God.</u>

I choose to let go. It's finally time to choose myself.

8

Stop the cycle of disrespect

A soft spot can create a bias that makes it difficult for a person to see disrespectful behaviour. Having a soft spot for someone may be causing you to tolerate behaviour that is disrespectful. Consistently overlooking disrespect due to a soft spot for someone can harm your self-esteem and well-being in the long run.

Respect is essential in all relationships - romantic, platonic or familial.

The impact of being disrespected in a relationship can linger long after the relationship ends. It can even lead to depression and anxiety.

The recommended course of action if you feel disrespected in a relationship is to set boundaries by standing up for yourself.

It is essential to remember that respect should always be at the heart of any relationship: Prioritize your self-worth and happiness.

9

Self-respect over Love

Respect is love in action.

Respect is a fundamental trait which should be given to people in general. It is the foundation of any healthy relationship.

What is Respect in a healthy relationship?

Respect is the freedom to be yourself and to be loved for who you are.

While it's important to respect people, it's also really important to have respect for yourself. Self-respect is the key to building confidence and maintaining healthy relationships with other people.

Why choose Self-respect over love?

Self-respect is much more important than having someone in your life because you can live without people but you cannot live without your dignity. Do not be afraid to lose people but be afraid to lose yourself at the cost of your own dignity, people will come or go as per their needs or desires.

While the feeling of passion, intimacy and commitment is important, respect is what keeps it all together.

To sum it up, respect is more important than love.

10

I Choose Myself over everything & everyone else

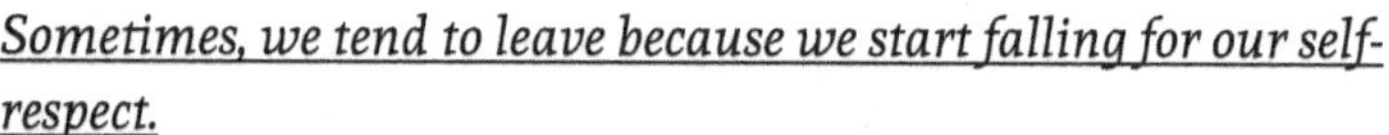

Sometimes, we tend to leave because we start falling for our self-respect.

What it means to choose yourself:

Choosing yourself means that you own your truth, step into your power, and, rise up to become the highest,best, and, most authentic version of yourself.

Choosing yourself means focusing on your happiness.

Choosing yourself means living life at your own pace.

Choosing yourself means navigating towards what adds positivity to your life without hesitance.

Choosing yourself means building a life that works best for you.

Choose yourself despite what others think or feel about it. Practice self-love.

11

What it means to choose Yourself

We are here to be real with ourselves.

Key Aspects of Choosing Yourself:

1. Prioritizing yourself by putting your own needs, aspirations and wellbeing at the forefront of your life- this can be portrayed in a variety of ways:

(a)setting boundaries by not allowing others to take advantage of you

(b)learning to say "no" when necessary by actively identifying and addressing your own desires and requirements

-by focusing on your own well-being, you can manage stress more effectively

2. Self-care - Treat yourself with kindness and compassion by engaging in activities that nourish your mind, body, and spirit, like:

(a)relaxation techniques, (b)exercise, (c)hobbies

-when you are happy and fulfilled in your own life, you can bring a more positive presence to your relationships with others

12

Choose yourself and They will too

You become a more fulfilled person, naturally attracting people who genuinely want to be a part of your life, by choosing yourself.

- The core idea is : You need to love yourself before expecting others to do the same.

This concept is about prioritizing your own mental well-being so you can be a better person overall.

13

Mental Health: Overview

Concepts in mental health:

Mental health is a state of mental well-being that enables people to cope with the stresses of life, realize their abilities, learn well and work well, and contribute to their community. It is an integral component of health and well-being that underpins our individual and collective abilities to make decisions, build relationships, and shape the world we live in.

Mental health is a basic human right.

Mental health promotion and prevention:

Promotion strategies:

1. Educate people about mental illness
2. Practice mindfulness i.e. practice being present in the moment
3. Improve your mood by regularly engaging in physical activity. Try to fit physical activity into your daily schedule
4. Talk to supportive friends and family members

-these strategies can improve mental health

Prevention strategies:

1. Identify people who are at risk of mental illness
2. Support people who are showing signs of mental illness
3. Work to destigmatize mental illness

14

Mental Health Awareness

Studies show a considerable percentage of the Indian population experiences mental health issues with depression and anxiety being common disorders. A significant stigma surrounds mental illness in India preventing people from openly discussing their mental health concerns and seeking help. Access to qualified mental health professionals, especially in rural areas, remains limited.

India has a relatively high suicide rate.

-Addressing mental health issues becomes crucial not only for the well-being of affected individuals but also for the overall progess and development of the nation

The World Health Organisation (WHO) defines "Health as a state of complete physical, mental and social well-being, and not merely the absence of disease or infirmity."

In India, while 20% of our population suffers from a mental illness, only 10-12% of them seek aid for their mental health concerns.

THE IMPORTANCE OF MENTAL HEALTH AWARENESS:

What is a mental illness?

A mental illness is an illness of the brain that causes disturbances in thinking making it difficult to cope with the ordinary demands of life.

What can you do to help?

A few powerful things you can do to help :

Acceptance by seeing someone as an individual and not as their illness, can make the biggest difference for someone who is struggling with their mental health. Learn about mental health conditions, symptoms and treatments. Reduce stigma by sharing your personal experiences and encouraging others to seek help.

Why is mental health awareness important?

It helps people understand that help is available

It helps people understand that mental illness is not a cause for shame

RECOGNIZING & ADDRESSING COMMON MENTAL HEALTH DISORDERS:

Anxiety Disorders- Anxiety is a normal reaction to stress but its chronic state may disrupt people's daily life.

These are common symptoms: persistent worry, restlessness, and physical symptoms such as dizziness or chest tightness.

Depression- Depression is a serious disorder that impacts a person both mentally and physically.

Symptoms of depression include feelings of sadness, and persistent, intense state of unhappiness. It might also result in loss of interest in all types of activities, loss of energy, and change in appetite or sleep.

CONCLUSION:

Thus, there should be mental health awareness so that people do not have to be embarassed or fearful about asking for help concerning their mental health.

One study found mental health literacy among adolescents to be very low, i.e. depression was identified by 29.04% and shizophrenia/psychosis was recognized only by 1.31%. These findings reinforce the need to increase awareness of mental health.

15

Treatment of Mental Health Disorders

Psychotherapy paired with medication is the most effective way to promote recovery.

Psychotherapy is a treatment that uses psychological methods to help people change their thoughts, feelings, and behaviours in order to help them overcome problems, increase happiness and improve their mental health. It is also known as Talk therapy.

Psychotherapy can be offered as a standalone treatment or alongside medication.

Mental Health Tips - backed by Research:

1. Get closer to Nature : Nature can have a calming effect on us.

2. Get more sleep : Adults need between 7 and 9 hours sleep a night.

3. Moving our bodies : Dancing, cycling, going to the gym - are great ways to improve our mental health.

4. Eat healthy food : A Balanced diet is essential for good physical and mental health .

5. Plan things to look forward to.

6. Talk to someone you trust for support.

16

Heartfelt Prayers for Mental Health

LOVING GOD, YOU ARE ALWAYS NEAR TO US, ESPECIALLY WHEN WE ARE WEAK, SUFFERING AND VULNERABLE. REACH OUT TO THOSE WHO EXPERIENCE MENTAL ILLNESS. LIFT THEIR BURDENS, CALM THEIR ANXIETY, AND QUIET THEIR FEARS. SURROUND THEM WITH YOUR HEALING PRESENCE THAT THEY MAY KNOW THAT THEY ARE NOT ALONE.

WE ASK THIS IN THE NAME OF JESUS, AMEN.

-The righteous cry out, the Lord hears and He rescues them from all their afflictions.

The Lord is close to the brokenhearted, saves those whose spirit is crushed.

PSALM 34:18-20

17

Opening Up about my struggle with Bipolar Disorder

Bipolar Disorder

also called : manic depression

OVERVIEW:

A disorder associated with episodes of mood swings ranging from depressive lows to manic highs.

Living with manic depression teaches you the importance of self-compassion, prioritizing self-care practices and building a strong support system.

Depression is a medical condition, not a character flaw.

Seeking help is a sign of strength, not weakness.

Recovery from depression is often a journey with small steps forward, not an immediate fix.

My name is Phidaribha Warjri, and my Pronouns are she/her. I'm in my mid-twenties. I'm the Author of the fiction Novella(s) : *'Her Testimony' & 'Her Story : The Prequel of Her Testimony'* and I am filled with immense joy to place

in the hands of the readers my third fiction novella : *'From criticism to Grace : Her Story'*.

Several years ago, I was diagnosed with Manic Depression, also known as, Bipolar Disorder, and I experienced an episode of psychosis. I saw and heard things that weren't there (hallucinations), and I felt overwhelmed and confused during the psychotic episode. I used to be terrified of what happened to me, however, with helpful resources, therapists, and along with the support of my loved ones, I have overcome the fear.

Overcoming Depression with God's Help: A Christian who suffers from bipolar disorder should treat it like any other physiological disease.

Because bipolar disorder alters a person's perceptions of reality, so, a strong foundation in truth, is a necessity when dealing with it, by finding Godly counsel (Proverbs 1:5) and spending time in God's word (2 Timothy 3:16-17).

Even though bipolar disorder tried to steal my life away, John 10:10 reminds me that I can have an abundant life in Christ.

18

To my support system: Thank you for loving me through my mental illness

To Anyone who's helped me through my mental illness, with sincerity and gratitude, I thank you all for being pillars of support, understanding, and strength, in my mental health journey.

My long journey with mental illness hasn't been an easy one. Suddenly one day, depression changed me into a different person, without warning. It's been rough for me and I understand that it's also been rough for the people around me.

So, if you've stuck around and helped me with my mental health crisis, thank You.

While others saw me as "Crazy", you saw I was hurting. Depression turned me into someone I wasn't; when I was hurting, I tend to do and say things I don't mean.

To those who could not handle it,
I am sorry. I truly am sorry.
To those who stayed,
Thank you. I love you.

19

Unconditional love : A Tribute to Mom

The only unconditional love in the world is the love of a Mother.

My mother is my best friend, she supports and encourages me in every step of life. She is my guiding light, she holds my hand through ups and downs of life. I do not merely love her because she's my mother but because she's my world. I learned the meaning of kindness from her. She's a beacon of love and strength.

I can never repay the priceless sacrifice and love of our Mother. She is the Super Woman of our lives.

Despite the challenges of single parenthood while also grieving the loss of her husband, our mother has been solely responsible for caring for my siblings & I, and, for raising us on her own.

My Mother, I Love You.

Enter Caption

20

A Tribute to my family

<u>My Grandparents:</u>

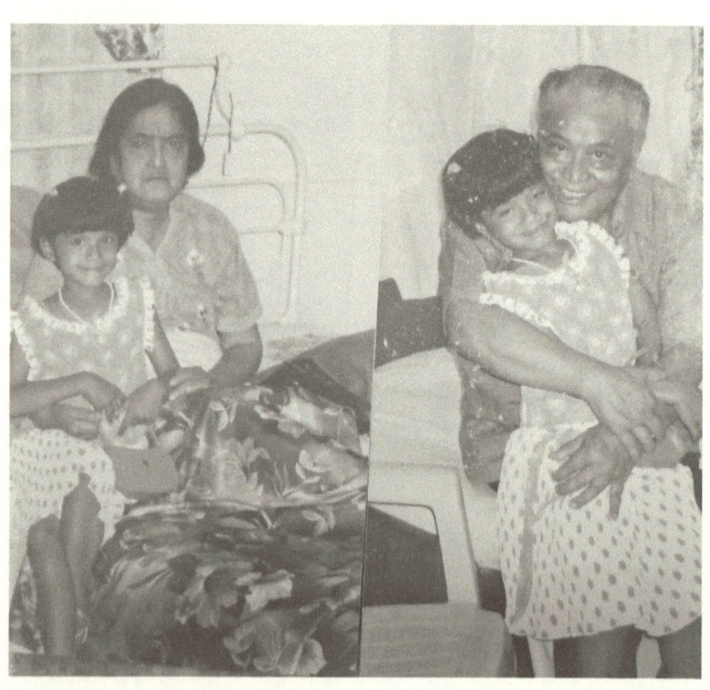

Enter Caption

As my paternal grandmother passed away when I was very young, I only remember a few memories of her. One thing I surely remember is she used to pamper me the most, however, she would also correct my mistakes and scold me when necessary.

On the other hand, my paternal grandfather seemed to be a Hero when I was a child. He was not only my grandfather, but, he was my spiritual pillar. He was a great inspiration to many.

The night that he passed away, my cousins and I, we remembered reminiscing on all the good times that we shared with our Grandfather. Losing him was indeed an extremely painful experience.

I am 27 years old now, but I was 17 when I lost my Grandfather. He was my mentor and the best man I have ever had the honor of knowing.

On 24th December 2015, I dealt with what felt like my first major loss. I knew he was gone, sure; I was sad, but I did not understand fully what death meant. Four years later, on 2nd November 2019, my father died suddenly, completely out of the blue, and when he died, it shattered my heart.

Losing a loved one can be very painful and can cause a feeling of disbelief.

Coping with the loss of a loved one involves:

1. Acknowledging your emotions

2. Accepting your new reality

3. Taking care of yourself

4. Celebrate your loved one

To my favourite aunt and uncle:

My favourite aunt, Aunt Aitinora & My favourite uncle, Uncle Sanlang - they hold a special place in my heart for numerous reasons that extend beyond the bonds of familial ties.

My aunt is a pillar of unwavering support, offering a listening ear when I navigate life's complexities & my uncle's vivacity and enthusiasm are contagious, making every family gathering an event to anticipate eagerly.

Their generosity extends beyond material gifts & their compassion extends beyond family borders.

I am truly blessed to have them in my life.

From Criticism To Grace

"***From Criticism to Grace***" signifies the idea to learn from criticism by paying attention to the perspective of the critic but not to let criticism control our response; to acknowledge its potential validity and using it as an opportunity for personal growth.

Cherishing One Of Life's Most Precious Gifts - The Gift Of Family

Family

"For where your treasure is,
there your heart will be also."

Luke 12:34

A Heartfelt Apology

To Anyone who's helped me through my mental illness, with sincerity and gratitude, I thank you all for being pillars of support, understanding, and strength, in my mental health journey.

My long journey with mental illness hasn't been an easy one. Suddenly one day, depression changed me into a different person, without warning. It's been rough for me and I understand that it's also been rough for the people around me.

So, if you've stuck around and helped me with my mental health crisis, thank You.

While others saw me as "Crazy", you saw I was hurting. Depression turned me into someone I wasn't; when I was hurting, I tend to do and say things I don't mean.

To those who could not handle it,

I am sorry. I truly am sorry.

To those who stayed,

Thank you. I love you.

From Depressed To Blessed

"Be thankful in all circumstances, for this is God's will for you, who belong to Christ Jesus."

1 Thessalonians 5:18

Never in a million years did I think I would be thanking Jesus for the very thing that took so much life from me.

I don't think I would be the person I am today without my depression.

Sometimes it's difficult to see the redemptive side of situations while we are in the middle of the mess, but that's exactly where our Faith has an opportunity to grow.

My name is Phidaribha Warjri, and my Pronouns are she/her. I'm in my mid-twenties. I'm the Author of the fiction Novella(s) : *'Her Testimony' & 'Her Story : The Prequel of Her Testimony'* and I am filled with immense joy to place in the hands of the readers my third fiction novella : *'From criticism to Grace : Her Story'*.

Several years ago, I was diagnosed with Manic Depression, also known as, Bipolar Disorder, and I experienced an episode of psychosis. I saw and heard things that weren't there (hallucinations), and I felt overwhelmed and confused during the psychotic episode. I used to be terrified of what happened to me, however, with helpful resources, therapists, and along with the support of my loved ones, I have overcome the fear.

On the other side of Depression:

2025 & I've regained my health and my emotional well-being.

Overcoming Depression with God's Help: A Christian who suffers from bipolar disorder should treat it like any other physiological disease.

Because bipolar disorder alters a person's perceptions of reality, so, a strong foundation in truth, is a necessity when dealing with it, by finding Godly counsel (Proverbs 1:5) and spending time in God's word (2 Timothy 3:16-17).

Even though bipolar disorder tried to steal my life away, John 10:10 reminds me that I can have an abundant life in Christ.

I am thankful for depression because it has stripped away judgemental attitudes and replaced them with great love, mercy and grace.

So with that, I say, "**Thank You Jesus.**"

www.ingramcontent.com/pod-product-compliance
Lightning Source LLC
La Vergne TN
LVHW090140160826
845673LV00017B/2534